Sid's War

Stories linking with the History
National Curriculum Key Stage 2

First published in 1998 by Franklin Watts
338 Euston Road, London NW1 3BH

Franklin Watts Australia
Level 17/207 Kent Street, Sydney NSW 2000

This edition published 2002
Text © Jon Blake 1998
Illustrations © Kate Sheppard 1998

Editor: Kyla Barber
Designer: Jason Anscomb
Consultant: Dr Anne Millard, BA Hons, Dip Ed, PhD

A CIP catalogue record for this book
is available from the British Library.

ISBN 978 0 7496 4604 2

Dewey Classification 941.084

Printed in Great Britain

Franklin Watts is a division of Hachette Children's Books,
an Hachette Livre UK company.
www.hachettelivre.co.uk

Sid's War

by
Jon Blake
Illustrations by Kate Sheppard

W
FRANKLIN WATTS
LONDON•SYDNEY

1

Evacuate!

It was Swotty Joan who found the labels. Buster Biggs pushed her in the stock cupboard when Mr Fisher was out of the classroom. When she came out she was holding up a square of linen with my name on it: SIDNEY KELLY.

"There's a big pile of them!" she said.

Swotty Joan was right. Hidden on a back shelf was a whole stack of labels, two for everyone in the class.

"What are these for?" I asked.

At that moment there was a roar from behind us. Mr Fisher was back, and he wasn't happy.

"Those labels are nothing to do with you!" he snapped.

"But, sir," I protested. "They've got our names on them."

Mr Fisher told me not to be cheeky,

even though I wasn't, and then backed down and explained.

"As you know," he said, "there is *not* going to be a war. But, *just in case*, the school is making plans to evacuate you."

It was the first time I'd heard the word EVACUATE. I didn't know what it meant but it sent my blood cold. EVACUATE. It sounded a bit like EVAPORATE. If you evaporate it means you turn into gas. Everyone said the Germans were going to gas us, which was why we all had big rubber gas masks. I looked up the word EVACUATE in a dictionary:

Evacuate:

1. Move people away from a place of danger.

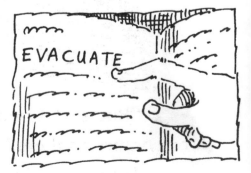

2. Empty the bowels.

So EVACUATE had two meanings! But which one was Mr Fisher on about? I needed answers fast.

"Sir," I asked. "Are we going to take it in turns to evacuate?"

"No, Sidney," replied Mr Fisher. "We are all going to evacuate together."

"Even the teachers?" I asked.

"Even the teachers," replied Mr Fisher.

"Sir," I asked. "Where are we going to evacuate?"

"Into the country," replied Mr Fisher.

I still wasn't too sure what Mr Fisher meant, but I found out soon enough. Next day there was a meeting in the church hall and a man gave a speech. He said that if a war *did* start (even though it wouldn't, of course) important cities were going to get bombed. So it would be a good idea if all the children and blind people and mums-with-babies got out quickly.

Dad had signed a form to say they could take me and my sister Rita. I was going to be torn away from Mum, Dad,

Gran and, even worse, my cat Tiger. Ah well, I thought. It was pretty bad, but not as bad as emptying your bowels in a field.

The Real Thing

Over the next weeks we started practising for this EVACUATION. We were put in teams of fifty and trained to march together and cross roads in an orderly manner. This wasn't easy when you had Buster Biggs swinging his gas mask at your

head. We had to carry our masks in cardboard boxes hung round our necks, and one day we all had to put them on. They were heavy and stuffy and stank of rubber, but at least they hid Buster's face.

Everybody had a haversack. Dad made ours out of old coal sacks. Every week Mum packed them with spare clothes and soap and towels and food for the journey. I don't know why, because we never went anywhere – just round the school yard or down to the railway station and back.

The summer holidays arrived, the weather was brilliant, Dad got called up to the army reserve and we forgot all about leaving London.

But we were in for a surprise. At the end of August we were called back to school and told to go home and pack. This time it was for real.

I didn't sleep much that night. I was even awake when the bugs came out of the wallpaper and climbed up in bed with me. In the morning I said goodbye to Tiger.

"I won't forget you, Tiger," I said.

"You're right there," said Rita. "Have you smelt your raincoat?"

I rushed to the door and grabbed my one and only coat. It stank. Tiger had been marking his territory again.

"Mum!" I cried. "The cat's peed on my coat! Do something!"

"Too bad," said Mum. "You've got to be in school in five minutes."

Mum wasn't the kind of person to get all tearful about her kiddies leaving home.

Some of the other mums, though, they were crying and wailing and going, "Oh my babies!" all the way to school.

We lined up in the playground behind two kids carrying a sign with our school numbers on it. There was a check of names, gas masks and haversacks. Then we were off, marching like soldiers, with a big trail of crying mums keeping to the rear.

Yes, we kept pretty good order, apart from one small problem. No one wanted to walk next to me.

"Sir!" wailed Robert Goody. "Sid stinks!"

"KEEP IN LINE!" barked Mr Fisher. "WE DON'T WANT AN ACCIDENT!"

"Sid's already had one," mumbled Kevin Palmer.

When we finally arrived at the
station, it was one great seething mass of
school kids, all labelled and haversacked
and grey-faced with anxiety. It was hard
to believe all these children were going to
find new homes. *Were* there that many
houses in the country? Were there *any*
houses in the country? I'd never been

further than our aunty's house in Hackney.

I'd never been on a train, either, and when I saw that great steaming monster I felt a mixture of utter terror and fantastic excitement. All around, mums were saying their last goodbyes, and as I boarded the train I caught sight of my own mum, waving frantically. As I waved back, she

began to cry.
I'd never seen
that one
before. I
wondered if she
knew something I
didn't.

"Sir," I asked Mr
Fisher as the train pulled
away, "if there isn't going to be a war, why
are ten thousand kids leaving London?"

"What *are* you talking about?" replied
Mr Fisher impatiently. "Of course there's
going to be a war!"

"Oh," I said. "That's
all right then."

I settled
back and
stared out of
the train

window. Parts of London I'd never seen, houses ten times bigger than our little terrace, then fields, trees, and . . . animals! Herds of animals!

"Look, Rita!" I said. "What

are those?"

Rita, who was trying to sit as far away from me as possible, glanced out of the window.

"Cows, stupid," she said.

"How do you know?"

"From an old book of nursery rhymes."

"Oh," I said. "Do you think they can really jump?"

"Eh?"

"You know, like over the moon."

Rita screwed up her face. "Have we really got to stay together?" she groaned.

3

Mrs Brown-Hat

The journey took hours and hours. The teachers told us when to eat our packed lunches but they couldn't tell us about where we'd be staying. They didn't know any more than we did.

At last we pulled into a station. A

dozen old buses were waiting in the gathering evening gloom. One of these took us down a narrow country lane and into a mysterious village with not much more than a church and a few houses. The bus stopped and they took us into the village

 hall, which was a bare and dismal place with the windows blacked out. That worried me. The reason for the blackout was so the enemy bombers couldn't see, but the enemy bombers weren't supposed to come here, were they?

Anyway, we were lined up and told to look our best. A man called the EVACUATION WARDEN told us to KEEP OUR CHINS UP and LOOK SPRUCE. Then the doors opened and in came the villagers. They strolled around looking us up and down, some trying to be chatty, others whispering behind their hands. I pulled my sleeves down to cover the bug bites, and tried to smile. But I wasn't smiling inside. I felt like a bit of rubbish at a jumble sale.

One by one, my friends got picked off
and taken away. Not me though. Every
time someone came near they took one
good sniff and moved quickly along.

By and by, a short, stocky
woman came into the hall. She had a
rough red face, a friendly smile, and dirty
gumboots. I heard her tell the man in
charge she was looking for four youngsters
to help her out on the farm. Immediately
Buster Biggs stuck out his chest and put on
the most pathetic goody-goody smile.

Imagine my horror when she went straight
up and picked him.

Worse was to follow. The red-faced
woman chose three more kids, and one of
them was my sister.

"But we're together!" I blurted out,
but no one seemed to hear.

The red-faced woman led her
new family from the hall, chatting
about horses, a motherly arm around
Rita's shoulder.

I felt very alone.

More villagers arrived, more kids departed. Soon there were just four of us.

Then three.

Then two.

Then me.

And all the villagers were gone.

"Oh dear," said the evacuation warden. "I did think there were billets for all of you. There's always *someone* who lets you down."

Just at that moment the door at the back of the hall flew open. A tall, stiff woman marched in, wearing a tweed suit and brown hat topped off with a feather.

"George!" she cried.
"*Do* forgive me!
We've had a terrible
hoo-hah at the
Women's Institute
and my timetable
is ruined!"

My innards
shrank. Mrs Brown-Hat
turned sharply towards
me. Her face dropped.

"Is this all that's
left?" she asked.

"I'm afraid so,
Jessica," replied the warden.

Mrs Brown-Hat's eyes flashed me
up and down, cold and hard as a till.
"Oh," she said. She moved closer, and
I think she was about to ask my name,

when a wave of shock and horror went over her face.

"What is that *dreadful* smell?" she cried.

"Cat's pee," I blurted out.

"Cat's *what*!?" cried Mrs Brown-Hat, even more shocked and horrified.

"We could ask Mr Porter if he could take another boy," blabbed the warden hurriedly.

"Not. At. All!" snapped Mrs Brown-Hat. "I shall make it my *personal crusade* to give this boy a carbolic bath, and when I've done with that I'll wash his mouth out for good measure!"

4

The Enemy

Mrs Brown-Hat, whose real name was Mrs Abbott, lived in a house called Orchard Cottage. I never knew houses had names, but then I'd never seen a house like Mrs Abbott's. It had its own gate and a front garden big enough to build another house in. There was an entrance hall which was as big as a room in itself, a sitting room, a dining room, a kitchen, a pantry, a room they called The Study, not to mention the bedrooms. There was even a bathroom and an indoor wc, which Mrs Abbot called The Lavatory. The whole place smelled of lavender, and everything was in such perfect order I was almost scared to breathe.

Mrs Abbott wasn't joking about the carbolic bath. Not only that, she checked my hair for lice and made me change. Then I had to take my coat into the

garage, where there was a real motor car, just sitting there, with a real Mr Abbott polishing the bonnet. He didn't say much, but with Mrs Abbott around, that wasn't surprising.

"I can't understand why he didn't wear another coat," said Mrs Abbott.

"Haven't got another coat," I mumbled.

"Yes, and I expect your father spends all his wages on beer," replied Mrs Abbott.

Next, I was shown to my room, except it wasn't called my room. It was called Colin's Room. Colin's ties were still in the wardrobe, and Colin's photo was in pride of place on the dressing table. Colin was away flying planes in the airforce, and, according to Mrs Abbott, he was the most perfect human being who ever lived. I

was not to move a thing in Colin's bedroom, and WOE BETIDE ME if there was the tiniest scratch on the furniture.

I went to bed that night the most miserable person on earth. I'd never slept in a room on my own before, and suddenly

I ached to be back with Mum, Dad, Gran and Rita, in a house full of noise and life. Downstairs the only sound came from the wireless, followed by Mrs Abbott getting angry about Hitler. I'd never met Hitler, but I had met Mrs Abbott, and as far as I was concerned *she* was the enemy.

5

Dream Cake!

Two days later it was Sunday 3rd
September. Mr and Mrs Abbott took me
to church and Britain declared war on
Germany. My spirits sank when I heard
that news. Now I would never go home, I
thought. But Mrs Abbott's spirits were on
fire. She said ENGLAND EXPECTS

EVERY MAN TO DO HIS DUTY, and gave me a huge long list of jobs to do, as if I was her servant.

I trudged through the day feeling like the whole thing was a bad dream. Mrs Abbott went visiting and Mr Abbott practised his golf swing in the garden, always with one eye on me. Then, just as my stomach was starting to rumble, Mrs Abbott came back. Under her arm was a box. She opened the box and lifted out THE CAKE OF MY DREAMS.

It was a dark, rich fruit cake with big swollen cherries busting out of the sides. On top was a layer of marzipan as thick as your wrist, and on top of that was white icing decorated with red and blue sugar flowers.

"This should cause a stir when the vicar visits," said Mrs Abbott.

She cast an anxious glance at me as she carried the cake into the pantry. Then

she went to the kitchen cabinet, took out
a key, locked the pantry door, glanced
at me again, and checked the door for
good measure.

On Monday we started school again.
We were back in our old classes, with our
old teachers, except we were crammed into
the hall of the village school.

The moment she saw me, Rita
rushed up to me. She was beaming all
over her face.

"We're having a *brilliant* time!" she
said. "Mrs Bosley lets us help out
with the
animals,

and I milked a cow on Saturday, and we
all sit in the kitchen and eat great big
home-made pies, and play games, and Mr
Bosley plays a fiddle!"
I tried to smile.
"What's your
house like?"

I was just
about to answer
when Buster Biggs
barged in. "Met
any *yokels* yet?"
he said. "Oo ar,
oi lives in the
country, oi do!"

"Oh shut up, Buster!" said Rita.
"You're ruining it for every one, you are!"

"You should come down the farm,
Sid!" said Buster. "Chase some piggies!
Hear 'em squeal!"

"I'll make you squeal," said Rita.

Buster ignored her. "What's your house like, Smelly Kelly?" he asked.

"Brilliant," I replied.

"Oh yeah," said Buster doubtfully.

"Got my own room," I said.

Buster frowned. "Your own room?" he said. "You lucky dog! I've got to share with two stupid yokels."

"And there's other things," I said.

"Like what?" asked Buster.

"Like . . . cake," I replied.

"We get cake," said Buster.

"Not like this cake," I said.

"Why?" said Buster. "What's so special about it?"

I just smiled.

6

Under Curfew

We all planned to meet up that evening, down at the river. Jimmy Nolan had got a big bottle of ginger beer, and Buster reckoned we could catch fish using a stick and a pair of cotton stockings. I was just looking forward to spending some time with my mates.

But I was in for a big disappointment. After we'd had tea (which Mrs Abbott called 'dinner'), Mrs Abbott told me I was to tidy Colin's room.

"But I'm meeting my sister!" I protested.

Mrs Abbott was outraged. "You do not leave this house without my permission!" she said. "And till school starts tomorrow you are UNDER CURFEW."

I told her that Mum never put me UNDER CURFEW, whatever that meant.

Mrs Abbott told me that while I was under her roof SHE WAS THE LAW.

"There's a war on now," she reminded me. "And we must all make sacrifices."

Maybe we could sacrifice *you*, I thought to myself.

Next day at school, no one could understand why I didn't go to the river.

"It was brilliant!" said Buster. "I was chucking stones at the fishes, and I got one right on the back"

"Yew, that's why the farmer chased us off," said Rita.

"Stupid yokel," said Buster. "So where were you, Sid?"

"Me?" I replied. " I had better things to do."

"Such as?"

"You couldn't even imagine."

Buster began to look frustrated. "Tell us," he said.

Mr Fisher rang the school bell.

"It's that cake," mumbled Buster, but I was already on my way to lessons.

7

Sinful Creature

That evening Mrs Abbott had an important committee meeting. She was on lots of COMMITTEES, like the FRIENDS OF ST MARY'S CHURCH COMMITTEE, the WOMEN'S INSTITUTE COMMITTEE, the EVACUATION COMMITTEE, and

the RAT GASSING COMMITTEE. No,
actually, I made the last one up. It's just
that Mrs Abbott is *obsessed* with rats, like
she's obsessed with lice, ringworm,
bedbugs and everything she thinks lives in
my underpants.

Anyway, this committee was meeting
in the next village which meant Mr Abbott
had to drive her. Mrs Abbott thought
about taking me along, but I think she
would have been ashamed to be seen with
me. So she left me alone, with the usual

list of jobs, and a SOLEMN PLEDGE to
be on my VERY BEST BEHAVIOUR.

I don't think I'd ever been alone in
a house before, let alone a mansion like
Mrs Abbott's. It wasn't long before I
started prying into all the corners I wasn't
allowed. I went in the study and I went
in Mrs Abbott's bedroom. Then I
prowled through the kitchen and my
eyes fell on the pantry door.

I could just *try* it, I suppose . . .

Blimey!

I couldn't believe it!

She'd *forgotten to lock it!*

Without a second thought, I picked up the cake carried it carefully into the kitchen and laid it on the table. My eyes feasted on its dark secrets. I brought my nose close to the glistening icing and drew a deep luxurious breath.

There was a knock at the door.

I jumped back.

Another knock.

I ran to the window and looked out. There at the door stood Buster Biggs.

"Sid!" he said, seeing me. "Let us in, will you?"

I opened the door. Buster walked straight in and looked around. "Wow," he said. "Posh, eh? Better than our dump."

"What do you want?" I asked.

"Just visiting my mate!" Buster replied. "So . . . where's this cake?"

"Ah," I said. "So that's it."

I led Buster through to the kitchen. His eyes nearly popped out of his head. "She made that for *you*?" he exclaimed.

"Sure," I said.

Buster sank into a chair, elbows on the table, panting like a dog.

"Gi'us a slice," he said.

"No," I replied.

"Gi'us a slice," he repeated.

"Can't," I replied.

"Course you can," replied Buster. "It's your cake."

"I'm saving it," I said.

"What for?"

"The end of the war."

" But that won't be for *weeks*!"

Buster jumped from his chair,

opened a kitchen drawer, and handed me a knife.

"If that's your cake," he said slowly,

"cut me a slice *now*."

I was trapped.

"OK," I said quietly.

As if in a dream, I saw myself slicing into Mrs Abbott's precious cake, handing the piece I'd cut to Buster, and watching him push the dark sticky mass into his face.

"Mm-glovely," he grunted, spitting crumbs all over me. "Aren't you having some?"

"Sure," I said. I watched myself cut another slice, and this time feed my own face. Just as Buster said, it was glovely.

"Cheerio, pal," said Buster. "See you tomorrow."

With that he upped and left. I sat there in a daze, unable to believe what I'd just done, but telling myself it was only fair. Why *should* people like Mrs Abbott have the luxuries while we had the scraps?

We were supposed to be on the same side!

My thoughts were interrupted by the sound of a car engine. In a blind panic, I packed the cake back into the pantry,

covered it with a cloth, wiped the table
and ran upstairs to my bedroom. As if
any of that would do any good.

For the next hour things were
strangely quiet – just the twitter of
conversation and the sound of the news on
the radio. Then, suddenly, there was this
almighty scream. Footsteps thundered up
the stairs. The door flew open and there
stood Mrs Abbott as I'd never seen her
before. Her face was a pale purple, her
eyes were bloodshot and her lips were
drawn back like a mad dog's.

"You . . ." she snarled, "you . . .
sinful creature!"

I backed into the corner of the room. Mrs Abbott pressed in on me.

"A thief!" she railed. "A thief under my roof . . . in *Colin's room*!"

I curled into a ball. Mrs Abbott got wilder still.

"You will suffer for this!" she cried. "Tomorrow morning . . . you will see . . . I shall make you *very sorry*, young man! *Very sorry indeed*!"

Mrs Abbott towered right over me.

"Well?" she snapped. "Have you got anything to say for yourself?"

"Please, Mrs Abbott," I murmured, "I think I've evacuated."

8

A Reward

That night I wrote a secret letter to my
mum, saying that if anything was to
happen to me please look after Tiger, and
how sorry I was for breaking the teapot. I
didn't know what Mrs Abbott might do to
me, but she'd already told me what she

would do to the Germans, and it wasn't very nice. I was prepared for anything.

Not a word was spoken at breakfast. Mr Abbott stayed hidden behind his *Daily Telegraph*, and Mrs Abbott's face was like stone.

Then, when it was time for school, Mrs Abbott handed me my haversack with all my belongings in it, grabbed me by the wrist, and frogmarched me through the village. She did not stop marching till she was in the playground, where she waited till the bell had been rung and we had all lined up. Then she marched me to the front and faced Mr Fisher.

"This boy," she said, "has committed an UNPARDONABLE CRIME. As a result I am punishing him . . . by banishing him from my house!"

I couldn't believe it! This wasn't a punishment, it was a reward!

Mr Fisher, however, shook his head.

"But we have nowhere else to put him," he said, "unless, of course, someone would be willing to swap places with him."

Mrs Abbott's steely eyes turned on

the crowd. Everyone seemed to take one step back.

"Would, er, anyone be willing to swap homes with Sidney?" asked Mr Fisher, doubtfully.

Suddenly an arm at the back shot up. "Me, sir!" came a cry.

I strained my eyes.

The arm was attached to none other than my great mate, Buster Biggs.

Mrs Abbott smiled. Buster Biggs smiled. But neither of them smiled quite as widely as me.

Evacuation

To try and cut down on the senseless loss of life during wartime, the government asked people who were not actively involved in the war to move out of the big cities and towns - the targets of the German bombs - and to stay in the countryside where it was safer.

More people were moved during the Second World War (1939-1945) than at any time in British history. Three and a half million were evacuated in the first twelve days of September 1939; by the end of the war the figure was more than four million.

Who was evacuated?

There were three categories of evacuees: schoolchildren between 5 and 15; pregnant women and women with small children; and blind and disabled people. Most of the schoolchildren went in school groups and were accompanied by their teachers.

London was not the only city to be evacuated. Many large cities including Birmingham, Manchester and Glasgow were also evacuated, as were ports such as Southampton and Portsmouth.

The cost of evacuation

The government paid 3 shillings per week for the upkeep of each evacuee. The evacuee's family was required to pay another 6 shillings.

No one was forced to evacuate. Many families chose to stay put – far more than the government had expected. City schools which had been closed down were forced to open again. Also, almost half of the first batch of evacuees had returned home by early 1940.

A second mass evacuation began at Easter 1940, amid fears of a German invasion. To encourage people, the government now paid £1 4s 2d (about £1.21) for each evacuee's keep. It became compulsory to accept evacuees, which created considerable difficulties for poorer country people in small houses.

Experiences and benefits

The experiences of evacuees were many and varied. Some, for example, did not live in houses, but in camps. Others, like Rita in this story, were luckier, and stayed in comfortable homes. In spite of being away from their families and friends, these evacuees had a better experience. In fact, some evacuees liked the country areas so much that they stayed on there after the war – though they weren't always made welcome.

One result of evacuation was that more people were made aware of the vast differences between the classes in British society. Better-off country people saw clearly for the first time the scale of poverty in the cities, together with the bugs and diseases this brought. Working-class people from the towns soon realised that the land they were fighting for was not really theirs, and that they would still be living in the same poor conditions after the war.

This new awareness led many people to demand better living and working conditions when the war ended. In a small victory for women, many men, left behind in the cities, learnt what it was like to do the domestic chores.

Pick up a SPARKS to read exciting tales of what life was really like for ordinary people.

TALES OF ROWDY ROMANS
1. The Great Necklace Hunt
978 0 7496 8505 8
2. The Lost Legionary
978 0 7496 8506 5
3. The Guard Dog Geese
978 0 7496 8507 2
4. A Runaway Donkey
978 0 7496 8508 9

TALES OF A TUDOR TEARAWAY
1. A Pig called Henry
978 0 7496 8501 0
2. A Horse called Deathblow
978 0 7496 8502 7
3. Dancing for Captain Drake
978 0 7496 8503 4
4. Birthdays are a Serious Business
978 0 7496 8504 1

TRAVELS OF A YOUNG VICTORIAN
1. The Golden Key
978 0 7496 8509 6
2. Poppy's Big Push
978 0 7496 8510 2
3. Poppy's Secret
978 0 7496 8511 9
4. The Lost Treasure
978 0 7496 8512 6